Happy Holidays

To Mr. Gilles Forhan.
V. T.

A big thanks to Clément, Élyse, Frédéric, Inès,
and an extra-special thank you to Thiên-Thanh
for his valuable help with colors.
V. T.

Published in 2010 by Windmill Books, LLC
303 Park Avenue South Suite # 1280, New York, NY 10010-3657

Adaptations to North American edition © 2010 Windmill Books
Copyright © 2007 Editions Milan, 300 rue Léon Joulin - 31101 Toulouse Cedex 9, France.

CREDITS:
Author: Amélie Sarn
Illustrator: Virgile Trouillot
A concept by Frédéric Puech and Virgile Trouillot based on an idea from Jean de Loriol.
Copyright © PLaneTnemo

Publisher Cataloging in Publication

Sarn, Amélie
Happy holidays. – North American ed. / Amélie Sarn ; illustrations by
Virgile Trouillot.
p.   cm. – (Groove High)
Summary: As the Groove Team prepares for a holiday show and a two-week school break, Vic
and Ed doubt their abilities as dancers.
          ISBN 978-1-60754-526-2 (lib.) – ISBN 978-1-60754-527-9 (pbk.)
ISBN 978-1-60754-528-6 (6-pack)
          1. Dance schools—Juvenile fiction   2. Boarding schools—Juvenile fiction   3.
Dancers—Juvenile fiction   [1. Dance schools—Fiction
2. Boarding schools—Fiction   3. Dancers—Fiction   4. Christmas—Fiction]
I. Trouillot, Virgile   II. Title   III. Series
          [Fic]—dc22

Manufactured in the United States of America

Groove High

Amélie Sarn

Happy Holidays

Illustrations by Virgile Trouillot

Skyview Books

an imprint of

WINDMILL BOOKS™

New York

Me: I'm Zoe. I'm 14 years old, and I'm living my dream: going to Groove High to become a choreographer!

Vic: Vic is my best friend. She's beautiful, blond, and always in high fashion. She is totally fun!

Lena: Lena is too cool. She's an athlete and a rebel. Too bad she can't get herself organized! She always keeps Paco, her chameleon, in her pocket.

Tom: Tom is also super cool. But he's super clumsy. He's got a thing for Vic, who is not interested in him at all.

Ed: Ed likes to seem mysterious and distant. But once you get him going, he's really sweet and a killer dancer!

Clarisse: One of Kim's two "servants." She does anything Kim tells her— usually nothing good!

Khan: Our yoga teacher. Also my favorite teacher at Groove High. He's funny, cool, laid-back . . . and handsome!

Table of Contents

Holiday Tales

Let's see, I have ten . . . fourteen . . . thirty-one . . . forty-five dollars left. I already bought Mom and Dad their gifts, but I still need one for . . . I drop my pen on my desk. I feel the beginning of a headache.

Aren't the holidays great?

Yes, I like the atmosphere, the busy streets, the cold, people bundled up in their coats, children with their hats pulled down, almost covering their eyes. The dazzling window displays, the smell of roasted chestnuts, the warmth of the season . . . great! The holidays are less than ten days away now. I'm going home to Mom and Dad, evergreens, a fireplace, hot chocolate. And I'm leaving Groove High for two weeks!

Groove High is one of the best dance schools in the

country. This is my first year here and it has been . . . the most wonderful year of my life!

Next weekend will be the first time I've been home since September. My life is here now. So much that it feels weird to think I'll be spending the holidays away from my friends on the Groove Team. It would've been a groovy Christmas with them. I'm going to miss them . . .

I glance at the columns of numbers I've written in my notebook. I love the holidays, but making a budget for gifts is quite a challenge. And not only the budget—ideas for gifts, too.

What should I get Vic? She is crazy about fashion, so I could get her a dress or some cool jewelry. These are good ideas, but she is so picky, and I don't want to get her something she hates. I can just imagine Vic forcing a smile and muttering, "Oh, thank you, Zoe, it's perfect!" When really she thinks it's hideous. The other day when we went walking downtown with our friends, she was really excited about this great imitation leather purse with metal studs. It was super cool, but also super pricey!

For Tom, I have a few ideas. He plays the guitar and loves music, and he recently started doing capoeira, so an album of Brazilian music seems perfect. Except, I have the same problem with him as I have with Vic. He knows way more about music than I do, I'm not sure what he already has, and I'll probably end up making a terrible choice . . .

I thought about getting Lena a stuffed chameleon. It would remind her of Paco, her real pet chameleon. (That's right, Lena has a chameleon named Paco! And he shares our room, which drives Vic nuts. Vic hates reptiles . . . but so far she has let him stay!) Anyway, I'm sure a stuffed chameleon would make Lena laugh, but where would I find one? Stuffed animals tend to be more traditional—bunnies, bears, giraffes. The other day I saw a soft, velvet rat. It was adorable, but I need a chameleon.

For Ed, who's a film fanatic, a great dancer, and the son of the famous choreographer Philippe Kauffman, I have no idea at all! Plus, I want to get something for Kevin, Ed's younger brother, who's a total pest but also adorable . . .

Honest, the holidays aren't good for my sanity. What time is it? Oops, nine-thirty already! Lights out in half an hour. After that, my friends and I joke that it's just like in fairy tales: Miss Nakamura, the dean of students, transforms into a dragon. I put away my list and start to get ready for bed.

Lena is reading a manga comic (she discovered the *Fruits Basket* series not long ago and she can't pick the fruits fast enough!). Vic is at her desk, studying as usual. She hardly ever stops. She's already at the top of every class she's taking, but she's never satisfied with her performance. She wants to be the best in everything she does. I, on the other hand, just watch. I'm too tired to read or study.

I decide to go for a quick walk in the hall to stretch

my legs. I like walking around school in the evening, when everything is empty and silent. It's so different in the daytime.

"I'm going for a walk, girls," I say.

All I get from my roommates are growls. Nice! It's like living with a family of bears.

"See you later!"

I close the door gently behind me. The thick carpeting muffles the sound of my footsteps. Hands in pockets, I walk down the hall. Yesterday, they installed a huge Christmas tree. We're supposed to decorate it tomorrow. It should be fun—everyone will bring an ornament or garland to add. I keep walking, past the cafeteria, which looks like a ghost town. Everything is shut down, like it's sleeping, waiting until tomorrow morning's breakfast rush. I keep going until I reach the dance studio. Oh no, the lights are still on!

If Miss Nakamura sees this, Jeremy will get in trouble. Jeremy is the school custodian. He's the nicest guy—the exact opposite of Nakamura. She's constantly reprimanding him and making him recite the school Honor Code. Poor guy.

I go into the room to turn off the light. I push the door . . .

"Ed! What are you doing here?"

Ed is hard at work. He doesn't even hear me. He spins, jumps, turns, all in the air. It's amazing to watch.

Suddenly, he sees me standing there. He stops. The spell is broken.

"Zoe! What are you doing here?"

Um, that's what I asked *him*. But I don't say that out loud. He doesn't seem to be in a good mood. I know he hates being interrupted when he's dancing. He once explained to me that when he dances, he feels like he's in his own world, and everything around him just disappears. This is why it's so unpleasant to be interrupted.

I mumble my answer. "Uh . . . nothing. I was walking and I saw the light, so . . ."

"I need to be alone," Ed says. "Get out."

Ed doesn't look good, and it's not the Groove Team's policy to leave a friend in need.

"Are you okay? Is something on your mind? Is it your father?"

Philippe Kauffman is one of the greatest chore-ographers of our time, and I am a huge fan. In fact, he's the reason I decided to become a choreographer.

Since I was five years old, I've collected everything I can find about him. I even have a poster of him on the wall of my room!

And then I met him. Philippe Kauffman is not quite what I expected. Very eccentric, very talkative, and obsessed with getting attention. It must be difficult for Ed to live with someone who is so superficial and self-centered. Unlike the rest of the Groove Team, Ed doesn't live on campus. He lives with his

father (the high-maintenance Phillippe Kauffman) and brother in a large apartment not far away. But Philippe Kauffman isn't home much. Between his world tours and his busy social calendar, he usually leaves his sons on their own. But he still has extremely high expectations for Ed. Philippe constantly tells Ed he's not good enough and that he doesn't work hard enough. The truth is, it's impossible to work harder than Ed.

Ed ignores my question. He raises his foot onto the barre and stretches.

"It's late," I say. "You shouldn't push yourself so hard. You'll wear yourself out and then . . ."

"What do you want?" Ed asks irritably. "Are you here to spy on me or what?"

"No!" I immediately exclaim. "Not at all! But if Nakamura finds you . . ."

Ed interrupts me with a fit of coughing. His whole body shakes violently. I take a step toward him but he holds out his hand.

"Just . . . cough, cough, cough . . . just go!"

"But Ed . . ."

"I said, go!"

Ed is completely doubled over. Before his face was

red with coughing but now it turns pale. I can see the dark circles under his eyes. He looks terrible . . .

"Ed, please. You need to rest. Anyway, Nakamura will be here any minute to check that the lights are out . . ."

"Get out!"

His tone finally convinces me. I'm stubborn, but I'm not crazy. Ed won't let me help him right now. But I'm not giving up completely. I'm going to talk to the rest of the Groove Team about what to do. We help each other no matter what. I step back into the hall, closing the door behind me.

It probably doesn't seem like it, but Ed and I

normally get along really well. Sometimes I think I'm the only one he confides in. I walk back toward my room, making as little noise as possible. When I open the door, the girls are in the exact same places they were in when I left. In fact, they don't seem to notice my coming in. I drop onto my bed with a big sigh. Still no reaction.

I sigh again, louder this time. Nothing!

I get up and rustle some papers on my desk, go to the bathroom, come back, sigh again . . .

"What?" Vic shouts. "Are you going to tell us what's going on or just walk in circles until we drag it out of you?"

Finally!

Lena lifts her head from *Fruits Basket* and looks at

me, one eyebrow raised.

"It's Ed," I say. "I found him in the dance studio. He's been working all night!"

"This late?" Lena exclaims. "That's crazy!"

"Why is it crazy?" Vic counters. "He's a hard worker. Plus, did you forget? We have a performance on Saturday."

Lena raises her book again.

"Ed works too hard," she says. "He's always the first to arrive in the morning. While we eat breakfast, he's already practicing."

Exactly!

"I agree," I say. "He's taking it too far. For the last two weeks he hasn't even been eating lunch. He dances straight from noon to one!"

"So?"

Vic glares at me. I wish I'd kept my mouth shut.

"I work through lunch sometimes," she says.

This is true. For a while now, Vic has been spending mealtimes in the library. She always says she's not hungry and that she has to prepare for exams.

"Maybe you prefer to waste your free time," Vic explodes. She feels personally attacked. "But not everyone is like you! Lena, you read manga all the time, and Zoe, you wander around in the halls. You can't imagine that some people care about their performance review and grades!"

She's right. It's true that Lena and I don't work as hard as Vic and Ed, but still, when I think about Ed coughing, looking so pale . . .

"You're not being fair, Vic," I say. "Ed looks really sick. I just saw him cough so hard I thought he was choking!"

"She's right," Lena adds. "Work is good, but we shouldn't let him run himself into the ground!"

Defeated, Vic rolls her eyes, shrugs, and goes back to her work.

The clock says 10:15. Nakamura will be here any minute. We'll definitely get a lecture!

Vacation, Dance, and Problems!

"**M**y parents still don't know whether they're taking a cruise to the Virgin Islands or renting a cabin at a ski resort!" Kim says.

We're in dance class with Iris Berrens, the head of Groove High and the classical dance teacher. Because of our upcoming show on Saturday— three days away, including today—Mrs. Berrens is scrutinizing us one by one, correcting all flaws in our technique. Of course, we're not supposed to be talking. We're supposed to warm up quickly and get to work. But Kim never shuts up. It's so annoying!

"And for Christmas Eve, my mother is wearing one of Balenciaga's latest dresses. I think my parents are getting me a racehorse for a gift this year. I'm sure it'll be a blue ribbon winner!"

Ugh, she makes me crazy.

"A ski resort!" Clarisse and Angie gush. They both worship Kim. "Oh my gosh, that sounds so exciting!"

"Where is the resort?" Angie asks.

"In Switzerland," replies Princess Kim (princess of snobs, I mean). "Have you been there? Famous people from all over the world travel there. European royalty, celebrities. Everyone important."

Clarisse is very impressed.

"You mean, you get to meet . . . movie stars?"

"Oh, for sure. Over breakfast, after skiing."

I can't stand this anymore. I need to concentrate, and if I have to listen to these snobby girls for one more minute, I swear I'm going to strangle one of them. You'd think I'd be used to it by now. Ever since school started, Kim Vandenberg—who is, I hate to admit, beautiful and talented—has been talking about her rich parents. Whom, by the way, no one has ever seen. And as if that's not bad enough, she's also decided her mission is to ruin our lives. She hates the Groove Team and spends all her time trying to get us in trouble!

Kim has a brother at Groove High. He's a third-year student. Luke. He's a show-off. Like his sister, he's beautiful and talented. And like his sister, he annoys me. Any time I run into him in the halls, he ruffles my hair and calls me Carrot Top. Ugh! But then again, sometimes he's really nice. Still, I can never forget that he's related to Kim the witch.

"What about you, Zoe?"

Wait a minute, is this real? Am I dreaming? Her Majesty, Kim, has condescended to speak to me?

"What are you doing for the holiday?" she asks, still using her snobbiest voice.

I decide to ignore her. I continue warming up my knees, which is important. Kim laughs with her friends.

"Silly me," Kim says, with a condescending look in my direction. "I guess I thought she understood English. Whatever, I already know what she's doing for the holidays. Sitting by the fire in her bunny slippers eating overcooked turkey. Hahahaha!"

This girl is such an idiot, I almost feel sorry for her. I stay silent. I'm bad with comebacks. Usually I leave it up to Vic to shoot back a scathing remark. But Vic is deep in concentration. I try to ignore Kim's laughter.

Anyway, I have more important things to think about. This morning, Ed greeted me as usual, but he looked terrible! And still, now, he's like the living dead. I want to tell him Halloween is over!

"Pssttt."

I raise my head. Tom is trying to get my attention.

"Are you okay?" he asks.

"I'm fine. What about you?"

"I'm stressed."

"Why?"

"Well, the show is coming up . . ."

"Right, the show on Saturday."

I'm so stressed about money and figuring out what to buy people for the holidays, I've hardly been thinking about the show or about final exams. Suddenly, an idea crosses my mind: I can combine the work with some fun.

"Hey, let's all go into town this afternoon."

That way I can get gift ideas for my friends.

"Miss Solis."

Tom and I turn our heads. It's Vic's turn to be scrutinized by Iris Berrens.

"Very good, Miss Solis. Straighten your back, yes. Perfect."

Vic holds a beautiful arabesque. Wow. I hope that when it's my turn, Mrs. Berrens praises me this much.

"One, two, three, one, two, three." Mrs. Berrens taps the rhythm with her baton. "Fifth position, temps lié, very good, now fourth position . . ."

Vic dances her best as Iris Berrens lists the steps.

"Temps levé! Pirouette!"

As usual, Vic handles it like a pro.

"Leg up higher, Miss Solis. I said a pirouette, not a U-turn! Keep going! Pirouette! Saut de chat! Glissade! Not quite! Please repeat the sequence. Pirouette, saut de chat . . . where is your head, Miss Solis? Repeat!"

And suddenly—disaster! Vic stumbles, falls, and bursts into tears.

"What happened, Victoria?" Iris Berrens stands stiffly, frowning. "Get up! Let's see that sequence again! It's hard work, believe me!"

Vic stands up. Without a word, without looking at anyone, she crosses the studio floor, opens the door, and walks out.

I am stunned!

And then I hear Kim's horrible laugh.

Stuffed Chameleon and Revenge

"Come on, Vic, this is silly. You can't stay locked in there all day . . . talking to a chameleon."

Vic lies on her bed, her nose pressed into her pillow. She doesn't move. One good thing: she has stopped crying. After her abrupt exit, Iris Berrens allows me to talk to her. But Vic didn't want to see me and just shouted at me to leave her alone. Mrs. Berrens had given me only half an hour, so I returned to class. When it was my turn, I did my best and Iris Berrens, as always, criticized harshly.

I admit, Iris Berrens has not always been kind with her words. More than once, she has made me cry. But today I'm thinking about Vic, and Iris's criticism doesn't bother me. Maybe I'm getting used to it. Anyway, I can't believe Vic's reaction. I've known her for a long time, and I have hardly ever seen her cry.

The last time was probably when Mary Duffy stole her boyfriend . . . in middle school!

When class ended, Lena and I went to see if Vic would eat with us, but she was crying inconsolably. I sat with her and tried to put my hand on her shoulder, but she pushed me away. And of course, she refused to eat.

This time, Tom comes with us. We try to convince Vic to come to town with us.

"Vic, it'll make you feel better," Lena insists. "We'll have fun. We'll drink hot chocolate."

"No," Vic replies, her voice muffled by the pillow.

More progress: she is speaking now!

"We can go to the jewelry store and check out their new earrings," I add.

"I don't care!"

My shoulders slump. She's as stubborn as a mule, my friend.

Tom is terribly disturbed by the state Vic is in. I may not have mentioned that Tom is totally in love with Vic. He has been since the moment he saw her.

Lena taps on her desk. The situation is beginning to annoy her. Patience is not Lena's strong suit.

Paco, who picks up on Lena's mood, crawls over and seems to sniff her fingers. (That is, if chameleons have a sense of smell.)

Tom paces the room, hands in his pockets.

This is too much for Lena. She stands suddenly.

"Cut it out, Tom! You're making me dizzy. Look, Vic, we're not going to sit here begging all afternoon. I need a break from studying, so I'm going to go hang out with my friends and relax. If you want to sit here crying all day, have fun!"

With that, she puts on her jacket, grabs her bag, and heads for the door. She puts her hand on the doorknob and looks back at us over her shoulder.

"You coming or not?"

Tom and I are frozen. What I really want to do is crawl under the bed and hide. Vic will not appreciate being talked to like that—even by Lena. Usually, Vic's the one who gives the orders. I wait for an explosion. But instead, Vic seems to be recovering. She raises her head. Her eyes are red and swollen, her hair a mess.

Lena stands firm.

"So?"

To my surprise, Vic stands up and heads into the

bathroom. We hear the water running and suddenly she's back, hair brushed, face (almost) back to normal. She puts on her jacket and picks up her purse.

"Ready?"

There's still one problem: Ed.

As always, he's in the dance studio working. Lena and I go talk to him.

"Hey, Ed, we're going downtown. Want to come with us?"

"Can't," he says. "I'm working."

"Maybe you should take a break," Lena says. "What's with you lately? You and Vic! You're flipping out."

"Just leave me alone. I'm work—"

Ed doesn't finish his sentence. He coughs violently.

"Anyway, I have a sore throat. I shouldn't be outside right now."

Lena heaves a sigh.

"Fine! Stay here! Work until you collapse! We'll have fun without you."

But this tactic doesn't work on Ed.

"Fine," he says. "See you later."

How can we respond to that?

Downtown, the streets are crowded. People of all ages walking, arms weighed down with shopping bags. The shops are decorated with garlands and lights. We're bundled up in scarves and hats. It's lovely! I've seen at least three Santas in the streets. Tom takes free candy from one of them, and Lena does the same with the one across the street. They come back fully stocked. Even Vic takes a piece, though she almost never eats sweets.

We stop to listen to a group of street musicians. A brass ensemble: trombone, trumpet, tuba, and a bass drum. They're doing their own take on Christmas carols. They wear red hats, gloves, and scarves. They're great! Not far away, a little boy dances along with them. The smell of roasted chestnuts fills my nose.

The holidays really are awesome.

Lena notices a store full of gadgets.

"Want to check it out?"

The four of us walk in. The saleswoman eyes us suspiciously. I know what she's thinking: kids who are going to touch everything and leave without buying anything.

The shelves are full of kitschy novelty items, each more useless than the last: a colorful Plexiglass candy machine, a cup with a bendable straw attached, plasma lamps that grow brighter when you put your hands on them. Tom loves it! I glance discreetly at the price tag. Ouch! Luckily, Vic blurts out, "This hideous thing? You like it? I think it's awful."

Tom turns red and abandons the lamp. (He can't love something if Vic hates it!)

"Oh, no, I don't really like it, I just thought it was funny, that's all. But I'd never want it, it's way too ugly . . ."

Poor Tom! When will he realize that he and Vic just aren't meant to be?

"Ooh, look at this!" Lena cries from the back of the store. "Stuffed animals! These are awesome!"

Tom, Vic, and I agree. There's a huge basket filled

with different stuffed animals. Lena digs through it excitedly. See! I knew I had a good idea.

"I can't believe it," Lena exclaims. "A stuffed chameleon! This is crazy, it looks exactly like Paco, don't you think?"

Lena waves a stuffed lizard with big green eyes and a long, twisty tongue. She's right—it looks just like Paco. This is exactly the gift I had in mind!

Lena looks at the tag attached to its tail.

"Oh, cool! It's only ten dollars."

Ten dollars . . . not bad. How much did I have, again? Forty-five dollars . . . I would still have thirty-five left over. I could just find something cheaper for Vic, Tom, Ed, and of course, Kevin. It might be tough, but not impossible! As soon as we leave, I'll slip back in and . . .

"This is so cute, I'm getting it!" Lena says, already on her way to the cash register.

Before I have time to speak, she's handing the saleswoman a bill out of her wallet.

"Is this a gift?" the woman asks, still sounding irritated. (Clearly, she understands the holiday spirit.)

"No, I'm going to eat it now," Lena replies in a deadpan voice.

The woman frowns, obviously wondering whether Lena's crazy or just joking. She shrugs and takes the money.

Lena pockets her change and takes the shopping bag.

"Ready to go?" she asks.

We head out. Lena is smiling, pleased with her purchase. Tom is still recovering from his mistake with the lamp, Vic is quiet, and I am desperate! I'll have to come up with a new idea for Lena.

"Can I see it?" Tom asks Lena.

"Sure."

Tom looks at the plush toy and rubs it against his cheek.

"He's so cute. What will you name him?"

This is what I like about Tom. He's a boy, but he doesn't try to act tough or cool or try to be funny. . . well, sometimes he does, but not in an annoying way. He's sweet and he doesn't try to hide it. I think it's great. Too bad it's not what Vic looks for in a boyfriend.

"I'll call him Paco," Lena replies.

"Come on, let's keep going," Vic says. "Let's go to Marlow's."

Marlow's is the largest clothing store in the city. It's also the most luxurious. There are four floors, thick carpet on every floor, crystal chandeliers, velvet benches for resting, and all of the sales-people smile and are super nice to their customers. For Vic, this is paradise.

The store's huge doors open automatically for us. We unbutton our coats and take off our scarves. It's nice in here. We wander among the mannequins and browse the clothing on the hangers.

"This is so cute!"

Vic holds up a cropped orange sweater. It's really stylish.

I have to stay focused. The whole point of coming downtown was to find gifts for my friends. I glance at the price tag and . . . am blown away. A hundred dollars for a sweater! There's no way!

"Guys, what do you think?" Tom calls. He's standing in front of a mirror, trying on hats and making faces. With each hat, he tries a different attitude: flirty, serious, relaxed . . . he's such a goofball.

Near the hats, there is a display of scarves and gloves. These might be more in my price range.

"Hey Vic, look at these," I say. I hold up a knit-ted chenille scarf. I've already checked the price—twelve dollars. I can do that.

Vic looks at it.

"Not bad," she says. "It would look good on you."

"Oh," I say. "I meant for you."

"You think?"

Vic takes the scarf and wraps it around her neck. She looks in the mirror.

"It's pretty . . ."

I cross my fingers.

"But I don't think it's in style anymore. I'm pretty sure it's from last year's collection."

"Oh, really?"

"But this one . . ." She picks up a large black scarf dotted with multicolored sequins. "Now this is super cool. Don't you think?" She drops the chenille scarf.

I answer in a very small voice. "Yes, it's nice."

"It would look perfect with that top I have, you know the one I never wear because it's too open at the back?"

I remember. I was with her when she bought it and I told her she'd never wear it.

"See, I could wear this over it, and it would cover my back . . ."

I'm not really listening to Vic anymore. I check the price of this scarf, the one that goes so well with her top. To buy it, I'd have to rob a bank.

"I already told you, I hate that color! Why would you even suggest it!"

That voice. It comes from the other side of the store. All at once, Tom, Lena, Vic, and I turn our heads.

Kim.

She stands in the middle of the store, surrounded by salespeople, her face red with anger. Angie and Clarisse sit quietly on a red velvet bench, watching the scene. Maybe they're just glad that for once their friend isn't screaming at them. At their feet are dozens of shopping bags from expensive boutiques all over the city. One is printed with the logo of a trendy sushi bar. Kim is obsessed with sushi.

She snacks on it the way I snack on M&Ms. I've even seen her eating it in class.

"Also, the shape of this blouse is awful!" she goes on. "Bring me something else, now! I am going to be wearing this in front of a lot of very famous people. I must find the perfect thing. It's crucial! I can't believe this is so difficult!"

Kim's hands are clenched into fists, her voice more shrill than I've ever heard it. The saleswoman scurries away, taking the "ugly" blouse with her. Another salesperson bravely approaches, presenting at arm's length the scarf Vic just tried on. Kim grabs it and throws it over her shoulders, admires herself in the mirror, and turns to Angie and Clarisse for their opinions.

Both hesitate to answer. I can understand why. If they say the scarf is ugly and Kim thinks it's cool, they are in big trouble. Same for the other way around.

"Um," Angie begins. "I mean, you can pull off anything."

"You're right," Kim says, turning back to the mirror. "I'll take it. Not for a special occasion or anything, but for everyday . . ."

The saleswoman returns with a heap of clothing on her arm.

"I think you'll find something this time," she assures Kim.

"I hope so," Kim says, "because as I said before, my dad has a lot of influence here. He's friends with the owner. I could have you fired with one phone call."

Without warning, Vic, who's been watching the whole scene, crosses the shop, heading straight for Kim.

On her way, she grabs a blouse from the saleswoman, and flings it against Kim's chest.

"Darling!" Vic screeches, in a crazy theatrical voice. "This color is absolutely perfect with your complexion. I see you've changed your self-tanner . . . it's still a little orange, but at least it's not as bad as what you had in Vail last winter!"

Kim is stunned. She opens her mouth, but before she can make a sound, Vic goes on.

"Oh, wasn't Vail absolutely divine, darling? But I didn't see your name on the guest list this year. That's right, the parties have become so much more exclusive. What a shame. We'll miss you! Oh, my gosh, wait . . . you didn't know? That they took you off the list? Oh, I'm so sorry! But it's for the best . . . oh, look at this dress, it's absolutely gorgeous, isn't it?"

Vic addresses the last sentence to the saleswoman.

"Um . . . yes, it is," the woman stutters.

"Absolutely!" Vic cries. "It's decided, she'll take it. But this scarf is simply awful. This she can't have. Well, darling, great to see you. I've got to run. I have lots more shopping to do!"

Vic kisses Kim on both cheeks, turns on her heel, and walks away. She passes us, winking, and sashays out of the shop. I'm blown away! Kim turns bright red. Vic has left her completely baffled. The sales-people stifle their laughter. I gesture to Tom and Lena and we walk out of the store, too.

"You were great!" Lena exclaims, catching up with Vic on the sidewalk.

Tom is just as excited. "That accent you were doing! I can't believe it! It was so funny!"

I join them. "My favorite was the self-tanner! It was perfect!"

Vic pretends to be modest.

"Well, we better go," Lena says. "I don't want to be here when Kim recovers and catches up with us!"

We make our way up the street, laughing.

"Oh, look!"

Lena stops in front of a window full of cute pajamas. An orange and pink pattern plus a great orange hat.

"Those are so cool, don't you think?"

I agree. They're great. But I like the ones in the next window even better—a short turquoise night-gown with lace along the edge.

"What about this one? What do you think?" I ask.

When I turn to my friends, I realize that Vic, Lena, and I all have our noses pressed against the window.

Tom stands apart, hands in his pockets.

"I don't like lace," Lena says. "It's too itchy."

I see Tom out of the corner of my eye. His face is the color of Santa Claus's coat.

"What do you think Tom," I ask. "Pink or turquoise? Lace or no?"

Tom turns even brighter red.

Vic can see that Tom's uncomfortable. A half smile comes over her face. She winks at me.

Poor Tom. Sometimes it's easy to forget that he's a boy—we hang out with him so much and talk about everything with him. But I guess I can understand that he feels weird talking about fancy pajamas with us.

"Um, actually I need to stop in the video game store," he says. "I'll meet you guys later if you want . . ."

I almost burst out laughing, but I manage to keep it together.

"Well hello, girls. Out for a walk?"

We turn to see where the voice is coming from. It's Luke. Luke "The Flirt" Vandenberg, Kim's brother. He comes up to us on the sidewalk with his friend Zach. They both carry shopping bags full of

gift wrap. And they're watching us, smiling. Luke glances at the nightgown I'm staring at. Now it's my turn to blush!

Then, of course, Luke reaches out, ruffles my hair, and says, "That's pretty, isn't it. But I don't know if it would fit you, Carrot Top."

And with these words, they're gone. I could kill him!

Deep Sleep,
Deep Trouble

"Therefore, we can say that Germany is geographically the heart of the European continent . . ."

I stifle a yawn. Mr. Kornik's geography class is putting me to sleep. Plus, I didn't sleep well at all last night. I tossed and turned in bed, with bizarre scenarios running through my head: me, torturing Luke Vandenberg . . . me with balloons under my shirt, which suddenly pop as I'm walking down the street . . .

I may not have mentioned this but I . . . well, I'm self-conscious about my figure. I'm not very curvy. It doesn't usually bother me that much. But I'm sure that's what Luke's comment was about! After yesterday's little encounter in the city, I hate him more than ever! It's weird, sometimes he's so nice! And other times he can be so mean.

Anyway, I'll just do my best to stay away from him today.

As for Kim, Vic's little show worked very well. She's been ignoring us ever since. I'm sure she's planning her own revenge, but for now, we're enjoying a break from her attacks.

But Vic still woke up very grumpy. She studied until two o'clock in the morning. To make up for the afternoon, she said. And though she's always so concerned about her appearance, she couldn't do anything about the dark circles under her eyes. Even makeup couldn't cover them.

Compared to Ed, though, she looks great. He is beyond exhausted, the poor guy. When we returned from our trip downtown (grrrr, I'm still mad thinking about it . . .), we found him in the dance studio again. We offered him some of the candy we got from the Santas. He had been working the whole time we were gone. He was sweaty and went into another terrible fit of coughing. We ended up making him go home by force. We were so worried that Tom asked Jeremy for permission to escort Ed back to his apartment, because we were worried about him getting back on his own. (And of course Jeremy gave us permission. He always helps us out.) This morning we looked for him at breakfast but couldn't find him. We looked everywhere and finally found him . . . back in the studio!

Lena, Tom, and I (Vic is off somewhere studying for her English exam) have been begging Ed to take a break, but he won't listen. He just tells us to leave him alone. Between him and Vic, it feels like my friends are in some kind of hibernation.

Speaking of hibernation . . .

The teacher is still going on and on about Europe. Lena gives me a nudge (I'm sitting next to her because Vic wanted to sit in the front row). Lena points to Ed. He has his head on his arms, his eyes are closed, and the way he's breathing suggests that he's asleep. As I said, Mr. Kornik has that effect on people, but this is pretty unusual . . .

Unfortunately, Mr. Kornik has a habit of wandering in between the desks to make sure the students are paying attention. If he passes by and sees Ed napping, he'll get angry. We need to wake him up . . .

Lena is thinking the same thing. She tears a piece of paper from her notebook, makes it into a ball, and throws it.

The missile lands: the first one hits Ed's arm, the second his head. No reaction.

"He must be really tired," I whisper to Lena.

I glance nervously at Mr. Kornik. If he catches me, he's not going to be happy. I need to be very careful.

"Pssst, Ed!" I whisper. "Ed!"

Nothing.

"Ed," Lena tries. "Wake up, the teacher . . ."

Mr. Kornik unrolls the map of Europe mounted on the wall. He turns to the student sitting in the first seat in the second row.

"If you would, Miss Solis," he asks Vic, who has been paying attention to every word he says. "What characteristics do the Mediterranean nations share?"

"Their climate?" Vic replies.

"Yes, very good. Their climate!" Mr.

Kornik approves. "What else? Miss Brown, do you have any ideas?"

Angie looks helpless.

I am, too. Mr. Kornik is making his way past the second row, coming toward the third.

"Ed . . . Ed, come on!" Lena keeps trying. She leans down in her seat, hoping Mr. Kornik won't notice her.

I tear a piece of paper out of my notebook and make it into a ball under my desk.

"Well, Miss Brown?" Mr. Kornik presses.

This is my chance. While Mr. Kornik is looking at Angie, I launch my projectile at Ed.

"Yes, Miss Vandenberg?" Mr. Kornik says suddenly. I glance at Kim, who has her hand in the air.

"I didn't mean to answer your question, sir, but I was talking to Ed the other day about Europe and he knew so much about it. I'm sure if you asked him he'd give the right answer."

What a brat! Kim, too, has seen Ed sleeping and now she's trying to get him in trouble with the teacher.

"You were discussing European geography outside my class?" Mr. Kornik asks, flattered. "What an excellent student. And it's very humble of you to allow your friend to answer in your place."

There's no time left! It's absolutely crucial to wake Ed up right now! I launch my ball of paper. Darn it! I miss!

"Mr. Kauffman! Can you enlighten us with your insight?"

Mr. Kornik turns to Ed, who hasn't moved at all. Mr. Kornik frowns. He is moving toward Ed in long strides. He reaches Ed's desk, puts a hand on his shoulder, and shakes him.

"Aggh!" Ed cries, waking suddenly.

"Mr. Kauffman, you were sleeping! You fell asleep in my class!"

Ed rubs his eyes and tries to pull himself together.

"You fell asleep in my class," Mr. Kornik repeats.

Ed blinks sleepily.

"What do you have to say for yourself, Mr. Kauffman?"

Everyone knows you should never answer a question like that. When the storm hits, the best thing to do is put your head down and wait for it to pass. But Ed's not thinking clearly . . .

"I was up too late working last night," he

mumbles.

"Up working too late?" Mr. Kornik roars. "I hope you were studying geography at least!"

I close my eyes. Don't answer, Ed, please, just don't say anything!

"No, not geography," Ed says. "I was dancing. This is a dance school."

Oh no. The storm is about to turn into a hurricane.

"Where do you think you are, Mr. Kauffman?" Mr. Kornik yells. He is beside himself with anger now. "This is first and foremost a school. You are not just

here to dance! You think dance is all that matters, Mr. Kauffman? You don't think people will mind that you are completely ignorant?"

Ed, white as a sheet, slowly stands up.

"Let people think I'm ignorant. I don't care. All I care about is dance." He crosses the room and walks out the door, slamming it behind him.

Silence in the classroom.

Hasty Decisions

Obviously, there's tension in the air. Yesterday Vic stormed out of class, and now Ed too? What has come over them?

This afternoon in the cafeteria, we couldn't find either of them. Vic is hiding out in our room and Ed is . . . in the dance studio!

Tom, Lena, and I are sitting on a bench in the yard, lost in thought.

"It's 12:52," Lena says suddenly, looking at her watch.

"We better get moving," Tom says. "Iris Berrens hates it when we're late."

I pause and think for a minute.

"I wonder if I should try to get Vic. She's being so weird right now, I don't know if she'll come with me."

Lena laughs.

"Being moody and weird is one thing, but skipping class is another. Remember, this is Vic, the perfect student."

I nod. Lena has a point. Vic is too obsessed with her grades to skip class. But my intuition tells me I better go check on her, just to make sure.

"I can go find her if you want," Tom offers.

I consider. I know Tom would give anything to be alone with Vic, but it's probably a bad plan.

"No, you're a boy. You're not supposed to be walking around the girls' hall. If Nakamura catches you, you're toast."

Tom sighs.

I continue, "I'll run up there really fast and then meet you guys back in the dance studio. See you soon!"

I don't have much time. I hurry down the hall, almost running.

"Miss Myer!"

Nakamura's voice surprises me so much, I trip over my feet.

"Where are you gong in such a hurry?"

The dragon-lady stares at me, eyebrows raised,

chin set, arms crossed, towering over me. A shiver runs down my spine.

"Well, Miss Myer? I'm waiting."

"Uh . . . I, uh . . ."

Nakamura taps her foot. I feel my throat catch. This is it. She's capable of removing my fingernails one by one, or hanging me from the ceiling by my feet (I saw this once in a movie), or of coming up with some even more horrible torture if I don't answer. Yet somehow I can't speak.

"Miss Myer . . ."

"Oh, Zoe, there you are. Did you find what I asked you for?"

Jeremy! Our custodian! He's a hero, throwing himself into the lion's den to save me!

"Mr. Martin!" Nakamura focuses her gaze on him.

"Oh, Miss Nakamura, I'm sorry. I didn't see you there. I asked Zoe . . . I mean, Miss Myer . . . to get me a . . . broom from the closet down the hall!"

What is he talking about?

"A broom!" Nakamura roars. "A broom! You ask a student to get a broom for you, when there are dozens of them in the kitchen? It's five minutes until class, Jeremy! A broom! This is not part of your job description. Watch yourself, Mr. Martin. You are supposed to be the supervisor of the whole maintenance staff. You uphold the Code of Honor and make sure your staff follows it. I spent an entire year developing that code of honor, and I expect you to know it by heart. Did you forget?"

As Nakamura continues her tirade, Jeremy gestures to me to leave. I understand now. He saw that I was in trouble and took the blame so I could get away. Thank you, Jeremy! Believe me, I will not forget!

I sneak away quietly, watching over my shoulder as Nakamura continues to berate poor Jeremy. I open the door of our room and see Vic lying on the bed, her face buried in the pillow. (This is the exact same position we found her in yesterday, before Lena convinced her to join us downtown.) I sit down beside her.

"Vic? What are you doing? It's time for dance class. You know Mrs. Berrens will be angry if we're late."

"I don't care."

Ouch! I didn't see that coming.

"What do you mean, Vic? Dance is your favorite subject."

"I don't want to be a dancer anymore!"

"What?"

"I don't want to be a dancer anymore!"

What is she talking about?

"What do you mean, you don't want to be a dancer?" I cry. I couldn't stop myself. Vic lifts her head and looks at me with big eyes. She is not used to hearing me raise my voce this way. That's usually her job. But I don't stop. I'm on a roll. It's been a stressful week, and I'm at my wits' end.

"Listen to me, Vic! I'm getting sick and tired of your crazy moods. Frankly, I've had it with you!"

"No, but . . ." Vic tries to interrupt.

"There's no 'but,' Vic! I've known you since you were seven years old and since then, you have been following your dream of becoming a famous dancer. Both of us worked hard to get into Groove High. You were sure that was what you wanted. And now, you're one of the best students in the classical dance class. You're this close to achieving your dream, and now I hear you whining like a little kid, 'I don't want to be a dancer anymore!' You're better than that, Vic, much better!"

Vic sits on her bed, looking at me with a pitiful face. She used to make the same sad face when she was a little girl with braids and bangs. She would sulk and finally start crying.

Her chin starts to tremble. We're not far from Niagara Falls.

"But I'm no good," she mutters, her voice trembling.

"No good? What are you talking about?"

"Iris Berrens never stops criticizing me. At the beginning of the year she complimented me once

or twice, but she hasn't done that in a long time."

I sigh.

"Consider yourself lucky that she even complimented you in the first place. She's never complimented me once."

Vic shrugs, as if this doesn't matter.

"Yes, but I was always the best!" she goes on.

"Remember at the Marie Court School? Ms. Kiriak once stopped me in the middle of practice. She said, 'Victoria Solis, you are an exceptional dancer. In all my career . . .'"

"'I have never met a young dancer so full of promise.'" I finish the sentence. It's true. Ms. Kiriak, our dance teacher at the Marie Court School, admired Vic completely. She never missed an opportunity to tell anyone who would listen how talented Vic was. It was good. Vic really needs to feel supported. Her parents have never understood how important dancing is to her. They think it's just a phase and that eventually she'll choose a more practical career. So Ms. Kiriak's support helped Vic believe in herself. But it also had a bad effect—Vic has almost never been subjected to criticism.

Vic sniffs. Someone needs to shake her.

I repeat myself forcefully. "Listen to me, Vic. I don't know if you know this, but you're being ridiculous. You're whining because Iris Berrens dared to criticize you? This is Iris Berrens! The star! Who danced on the finest stages in the world and was famous all over the globe! And whose one goal is to help you become the very best dancer you can be! What is your dream, Vic? To always stay at the same level and wait for compliments from the eighth grade dance teacher? Or to make it into the New York City Ballet, or the Bolshoi in Moscow?"

Vic stares at me. She's listening to every word. I'm sure she's imagining herself dancing with a world-famous company.

I keep going. "You aren't at the Marie Court School anymore, my friend! If you want to get better, you have to learn to accept criticism. Besides, when . . ."

I don't finish my sentence because the door has suddenly opened. It's Tom.

"Hey, are you girls crazy or what? Mrs. Berrens noticed you weren't in class. She hasn't said anything, but I can see she's not happy. I had to talk her into letting me come look for you. I said I was worried—that it wasn't like you to be late and that I would make sure everything was okay."

Vic slumps. I get up and hold out my hand.

"Come on, let's go."

She sighs and takes my hand.

"Good luck finding an excuse," Tom says. "I don't think Mrs. Berrens is going to buy it."

I think quickly.

"You know what, Tom, go back to class. We'll go to the nurse's office and say Vic has a stomachache. This way, we'll have a note explaining why we're late."

Tom nods. "Okay."

Tom rushes out of the room. I look at Vic. With her eyes so red and swollen, we'll have no problem convincing the nurse that she's sick.

We close the bedroom door and walk down the hall toward the nurse's office. Vic doesn't open her mouth. I know how she feels. Next time I have trouble accepting Iris Berrens's criticism, I should give myself the speech I just gave Vic.

Ambulance in the Night

It's 11:00. Lena and I are in the room we've reserved in the library, where we meet to talk about our online magazine, *Groove Zine*. We nibble on cookies and chat.

Vic followed my advice exactly. She decided to keep studying to be a dancer. Thank goodness. Except that right after dinner (where she ate almost nothing), she joined Ed in the dance studio. I thought she would have needed a little rest, but instead she turned to me and said, "You know, Zoe, you were right. I needed a wake-up call. This isn't the Marie Court School anymore. I want to be the best I can be, so I have to work my absolute hardest."

I sighed and didn't reply. Vic is incredibly stubborn. I've always known that.

Lena breaks off a small piece of cookie and reaches out to Paco, who is crawling around on the table. He comes to investigate (chameleons are picky eaters?), then turns his head. No, the cookie isn't his thing.

"I can't make him eat anything but dead crickets," Lena says. "The other day, I saved him some chocolate pudding from the cafeteria, and he wasn't interested at all."

I don't ask how Lena managed to bring Paco the chocolate pudding (in her pocket?), because I'm still thinking about the same problem I've had all week: What gifts should I get my friends for Christmas? Lena has been keeping the stuffed chameleon on her bed and every time I see it, I feel desperate.

I take advantage of this time alone with Lena to see if she'll drop any hints. But I must be clever. I can't ask obvious questions, or she'll know what I'm doing. I start by bringing up the topic of the holidays in general.

"Hey, Lena, what are you doing for the holidays this year?"

"Oh, cool! Did you see? Paco just ate some of the cookie!"

I couldn't care less about Paco and his cookie. But I play it smart.

"Hey, what are you going to do with Paco over the holiday break? You said your parents don't know about him, right? That won't be easy . . ."

Lena shrugs.

"Mmmm," she says.

What kind of answer is that? I'm going to have to try harder.

"This year, my mom says she's cooking a bunch of different dishes," I say. "Sweet, savory, lots of different things to try. And she says we can eat them in

any order we want. Cool, right?"

"Mmmm."

Lena is preoccupied with Paco, luring him with cookie crumbs. She doesn't raise her head. There's something wrong.

"What about you, what have your parents planned? Are you going to see family? Friends?"

Lena heaves a sigh.

"Oh, you know, I don't really care about the holidays, so . . ."

I know this isn't true. I know Lena loves the whole holiday season, the decorations, the lights, the garlands . . . why is she acting this way?

"But I thought . . ." I don't finish my sentence. For the second time today, I'm interrupted by a door opening. Not Tom this time, but Vic wearing her dance clothes. She looks scared.

"Come quick! Please! It's Ed, he's not okay. I don't know what to do."

Lena and I jump up.

"What happened? Where is he?"

"He's coughing and coughing and he can't stop. It's like he's choking."

"Go back and stay with him," Lena orders.

"I'll get Jeremy."

When we get back to the dance studio, Ed is sitting on the floor, leaning against the mirror. He clutches his stomach and his face is pale. His eyes are bright, like he has a fever. His breathing is shallow and wheezy. I rush over to him.

"Give me a pillow!"

Vic looks around.

"Now!"

As fast as she can, she runs to the locker room and returns with a ball of clothes. I lift Ed's head and slip the pile of clothes under his neck to support his head. Vic sits next to him and takes his hand. She speaks softly. Suddenly, he starts coughing again. He closes his eyes. His face is tense with pain.

"What is going on here?"

Nakamura. She bursts into the dance studio, followed by Tom and Lena.

Lena approaches me and whispers in my ear. "Sorry! When I knocked on Jeremy's door, Nakamura was in the halls. So . . ."

I nod. Nakamura comes toward us.

"I see, the little team is all here. What are you up to this time?"

Nakamura thinks we're all troublemakers. For her, the Groove Team is some kind of organized crime ring!

"Ed is sick, ma'am," Vic says. "He needs a doctor!"

Heartless Nakamura looks at Ed.

"Mr. Kauffman," she cries. "Stand up now! I know this is some kind of joke! You must think I was born yesterday. I've seen it all, believe me."

If we let her keep going, in two seconds she'll be grabbing Ed by the collar. I get up and run into the hall. I race up the stairs to the fourth floor. In less than two seconds, I'm at Khan's apartment. (Khan is the school's yoga teacher) I knock and the door opens. Khan is barefoot, wearing a white tunic and pants. He was probably in the

middle of meditating. I don't give him time to ask me what's wrong, I just start talking.

"Something's wrong! Ed is in the dance hall, he can hardly breathe."

Khan reacts immediately.

"Let's go!"

Farther down the corridor, another door opens. Iris Berrens emerges, wearing a long silk dress, almost like a ghost. She smoothes her hair.

"What is happening?"

"Come with us," Khan calls.

All the commotion has brought a few students to the door of the dance studio. Jeremy prevents them from coming in.

Outside, an ambulance siren blares.

"I called the hospital," Jeremy says.

I want to hug him!

But when I go back into the dance studio, I hear Khan whisper to Iris, "He's lost consciousness."

Tears run down my face.

Reconciliation

We stay up all night talking. In all the chaos, Tom has no problem sneaking up to our room to sleep on our floor. We've made him a bed with pillows and extra blankets. It's probably not very comfortable, but what difference does it make? We can't sleep.

The paramedics immediately put Ed on respiratory support and carried him out to the ambulance on a stretcher. Khan went with them to the hospital. We watched the flashing lights until they had disappeared in the night. It was Iris who finally made us come in. Nakamura and Jeremy had gotten the other students to go back to their rooms. Iris said not to worry.

"As soon as we have news, we'll tell you. I promise."

Now we're up in our room, trying to guess what exactly happened. Poor Ed is the only thing we can think about.

"He couldn't stop working. He was in the dance studio from early morning until late at night," Lena says.

Tom and I agree. Vic doesn't respond. I look her in the eye.

"Ed can't settle for just good," I say. "He has to be perfect. That's the problem! He puts too much pressure on himself. Work is like anything else—you can't overdo it!"

Vic sighs and shakes her head.

"I guess you'd say the same thing about me, right?"

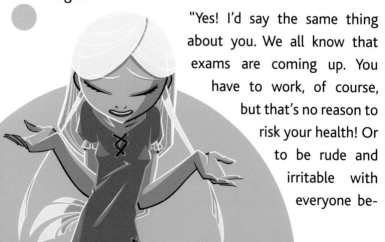

"Yes! I'd say the same thing about you. We all know that exams are coming up. You have to work, of course, but that's no reason to risk your health! Or to be rude and irritable with everyone because you're so exhausted!"

"I think Ed wants his father to be proud of him," Tom puts in.

Tom is smart. He knows Vic and he knows that if he doesn't change the subject quickly, the conversation will turn into a fight.

"He's said that to me before," Tom continues. "He wishes his father would say nice things to him, that he knows he's going to be a good dancer."

"But Ed is a good dancer!" Lena exclaims. "He's the best dancer in our class!"

We've been going on like this all night.

The alarm is about to ring and we haven't slept at all. Tom quietly slips back to his room to change.

Things feel grim. People are talking, but in hushed voices.

When we take our places in the cafeteria, all eyes are on us. Everyone knows Ed is our best friend. We eat quickly. (None of us is very hungry, not even Tom, which is a first!) Then we go out in the courtyard. Our first class this morning is yoga. Khan looks tired. He probably didn't get much sleep either.

"Good morning, everyone. Let's begin. I imagine none of you are really in the mood for yoga after what happened last night. You probably want to know how your friend is doing."

This is directed especially at us, the Groove Team. Khan looks at us as he says the last part. We don't reply.

Khan continues, "Ed had a severe asthma attack. This morning, the doctors took him off respiratory

support. He feels much better. Of course, he needs some rest and needs to stay in the hospital so the doctors can watch him. But he should be back to normal soon. Friends are allowed to visit him. If you like, I can take a small group to the hospital while the rest of you stay here and practice your dances for the show."

Without consulting each other, Tom, Lena, Vic, and I all get up and move toward Khan. We can see that he understands.

"Perfect," he says. "Let's go."

The nurses make it very clear that Ed needs to rest and that we can't wear him out. When we go into his room, he opens his eyes. His head is propped up on a pillow and he is still very pale. But not nearly as bad as last night!

"Hi," he says in a weak voice.

"You scared us!" Tom says.

"Well, at least now you have to rest," Lena tries to joke.

Ed gives us a faint smile. He still seems a little sore when he breathes. To keep from getting too upset, I say, "Hey, if you think you're off the hook for your *Groove Zine* article, you're wrong! As soon as you get out of here I'm going to need it!"

"Don't worry, Madame Editor," Ed manages to say. "You'll get your article."

After a pause, he adds, "Hey, doesn't Zoe sort of remind you of Nakamura these days? Soon she'll be making the Groove Team recite the code of honor. Just wait!"

This makes me happy. If Ed's sense of humor is back, I know he'll recover soon. He coughs a bit before continuing.

"Listen, I want to apologize for making you put up with me the past few days. Thank you for being there for me . . . as always . . . I . . ."

"Well, this is quite a reunion!"

A nurse enters the room. She walks up to Ed and straightens his pillow.

"All right, young man. I think it's time to wrap up the visit. You've been talking too much. And your father is waiting outside."

Ed grimaces. I don't know if it's the pain or the thought of seeing his father.

The nurse leads us to the door. Khan stays behind in the room.

"Don't worry," he says. "Tomorrow you'll get to

see your friend again. The nurse just wants to make sure he gets plenty of rest."

We pass Philippe Kauffman as he enters. He doesn't look at us.

The door has barely closed and I'm already pressing my ear against it. I hear snippets of conversation, something like: "Ed . . . okay . . . Yes, Khan . . . thank you . . . aware . . . you must take better care of yourself, son . . . better soon . . . work . . . health . . ."

It sounds positive. Either way, I have to quit listening, because the nurse is looking at me impatiently. She tells us we should wait in the hall until our teacher comes out.

Fine with me! Ed's going to be okay!

Welcome Back, Edward!

That night, I sleep like a log. I guess I'm catching up from the night before. After we returned from the hospital, Iris Berrens announced that, in light of recent events, she was postponing the final show and all our final exams until the beginning of January. What a relief! I'm behind in my classes. Khan told us Ed would be returning the following day, so we started organizing a welcome-home party. And later that day, after the mail was delivered, I witnessed another mini-drama. Kim was waiting impatiently for a letter, but after she read it she ran out of the room, and I'm pretty sure she was crying. Her brother Luke ran after her.

I'm dying to know what happened!

But this morning, I have something else on my mind. I think I've come up with a solution to my holiday gift problem. My plan is . . .

"We figured it out!"

The door opens and Lena and Vic burst in. I barely have time to cover up what I'm doing. I throw a sweater over my desk.

"Kim is hysterical," Vic says.

Lena agrees. "We were passing by the girls' bathroom and we overheard Kim and Luke talking!"

"Luke was in the girls' bathroom?"

Vic shrugs.

"That's where Kim went to hide after she got that letter."

"The letter was from her parents," Lena continues. "They're not going to spend the holiday break with her."

"Wow," I say. "After all her bragging about

Switzerland and celebrities. Serves her right."

Lena frowns.

"Actually, it's kind of sad," she says.

She drops onto the bed. She seems really upset about Kim's story. Vic and I ask her what's wrong.

"The same thing happened to me," Lena mumbles. "I'm not spending the holidays with my parents. They're sending me to stay with my aunt, whom I hate . . ."

"But why?" Vic asks.

"My mother sent me a long letter. She and my dad are probably getting a divorce."

Lena's eyes are full of tears. Vic and I each sit on one side of her and take her hands.

"Why didn't you tell us?"

I say softly.

"I couldn't," Lena sniffs. "It makes me too sad to talk about it."

Vic and I hug Lena. Now I see why she was so evasive about her holiday plans.

But I think I know what will make her feel better . . .

Welcome back, Edward!

We hang the huge banner in the middle of the hall. Everyone joins us welcoming Ed back. He looks almost normal again—still a little pale, but much better than before. He tells us that Khan offered to teach him a breathing technique to help him manage his stress and his asthma.

Under the banner, there's an amazing spread of food. We celebrate everything at once: Ed coming back to Groove High, the holidays, and the beginning of break!

I know it's hard to believe, but Luke is dressed like Santa Claus and is going around handing out candy!

When the party is over, I hand out gifts to my

friends. Like I said, I figured out what to do. I've made a drawing of each of them: Vic in the middle of a dance performance, Tom playing guitar, Lena playing with Paco, Ed with . . . his dad.

Just now, right before the party, I saw Khan with a gift in his hands. You know me, my curiosity always gets the better of me, so I followed him. Discreetly, of course. He went and knocked on Iris Berrens's door. So cute, don't you think?

I also called my mother earlier this afternoon. I asked if I could invite Lena home for the holidays, and she said yes! She called Mr. and Mrs. Robertson herself. I know my mother—she can persuade anyone. The Robertsons won't be able to refuse.

This vacation is going to be a blast!

"Hey, Zoe!"

Tom comes up to me and hands me a wrapped gift.

"Someone wanted me to give you this."

"Really? Who?"

"Open it and you'll see . . ."

I open the gift. A sketchpad! It's great, but I still don't know who it's from. There's no card . . . I open the cover. There's an inscription.

Happy Holidays, Carrot Top!

Luke!

I feel my cheeks turning red. I don't get this boy at all!

And I'm not sure whether I hate him anymore . . .

At least Lena and I will have plenty of time to chat about him when she's at my house for the break . . .

GROOVE zine ★

Edited
by the Groove Team

The holidays are always a headache. How do you buy gifts for friends and family, when your wallet is empty? Asking the right questions can help. What makes your friends happy? Think of a special gift perfect for each of them. It's better to use your imagination than to spend a fortune on items they might not like. The holidays are a great time to find a way to say to your friends and family: "I'm glad to have you in my life!" Remember, your friends still need you ...and not just for holiday presents!

 Zine #5 | All the News at Groove High

Welcome Home, Ed!

Once again, another party held at Groove High was a big success! It helped that we all had a good reason to celebrate: the return to school of Edward Kauffman, a promising young dancer in his first year. The buffet was perfect and we certainly ate well. But let's also remember Tom's excellent music, which allowed us to dance until dawn!

by Zoe

Dazzling Designs

The holidays can be a magical time. This is the time of year where you can afford to be daring with accessories and accents like rhinestones, feathers, sequins, etc.

You can easily and efficiently customize even the most basic of outfits, to add some holiday dazzle. Ideas:
- Glue or sew the sequins on a black top.
- Sprinkle a little gold glitter on a dress.
- Wear a boa.
- Remember, your makeup can also shine with a thousand lights and there are glitter-sprays for your hair!

by Vic

Sports Page

Breathe

Any sport starts with learning good breathing ... try to run the 100-meter dash or to beat the record for long jump without good breath control, and you will see! I think the best technique out there today is the method of yogis. Try it!

Sit cross-legged, inhale slowly inflating the abdomen, then exhale letting the air escape from your lungs. Repeat several times.

This system allows you to relax and increase the resistance of your lungs! And it's always good to have your lungs working at top capacity, right?

by Lena

Modern Christmas Sounds

The right music can really get a holiday party started! It can be fun to listen to some classic Christmas carols revisited. For example, you could check out...
- "Little Father Christmas" by The Black Spiders, kings of metal
- "My Beautiful Christmas Tree", hip-hop style by McDouble

The holidays are a great time to enjoy all kinds of music. Try to find the music that provides the "soundtrack" for all different festivals and celebrations like Diwali, Hanukkah, Christmas, Kwanzaa and the Chinese New Year. Check out the different styles of music! Music helps any celebration!

★ ★ ★

by Tom

CINEMA

The Nightmare Before Christmas

A Christmas movie not to miss! Forget the sweet, cloying Christmas movies you're used to, this animated film by Tim Burton (the magician of the cinema) is a masterpiece of humor and poetry! Jack, the scarecrow mayor of Halloween Town discovers Christmas Town. Back home, he tries to explain to his morbid friends the concept of Christmas, gifts and kindness! Really unique...and a great film!

by Ed

HOROSCOPE by Zoe

Aries
Uranus, Saturn, and Jupiter are watching your sign, just like that! This certainly bodes well for exams!

Taurus
Work, work, work! At this time, you only know that word! But don't forget to slow up the pace a little from time to time!

Gemini
Do not let your problems run your life! You know what they say: "There is always a solution!" Dig deep and you'll find it.

Cancer
Is it worth it to worry about vacation? Waffling between skiing and the beach! Don't spend too much time planning—things rarely go as planned.

Leo
You think everything always works out perfectly for you. This time, you may be surprised, so you should probably study a little more for exams!

Virgo
Yes, your friends love you. Yes, they think about you. Wait a bit and they will prove it to you.

Libra
You will have the opportunity to enjoy your surroundings while having a good time but don't miss the boat!

Scorpio
Things are tough at the moment and everythinG is falling apart. Don't worry, it's Jupiter's fault. Stand firm, it will not last, and after the rain comes beautiful skies.

Sagittarius
For you, everything is going great! Love, friendship, and health are all in order. Be glad things are going well for you, but think about others, too.

Capricorn
The stars are undeniable: you're in love! You haven't realized it yet? Patience, you'll make the discovery soon enough!

Aquarius
Keep things in perspective. The period ahead will be full of emotions of all kinds. Hang on!

Pisces
Stop putting pressure on yourself. Learn to relax. You do not have to be perfect!

Our School

Here is the west wing, with offices on the first floor; on the second floor are the boys' dorms.

The small park is for yoga classes or a place to relax after class.

Miss Nakamura's office. Note the view of the courtyard: escape is impossible!

The room that Tom, Luke, and Zach share.

The central building, with large dance halls, the main cafeteria, and the private apartments of permanent teachers (Mrs. Berrens, Khan).

Basketball courts and soccer fields. You can find Lena there!

Here is the pool.

Ed lives in this direction, 10 minutes by bus.

Iris Berrens's office.

Our room.

The east wing, with the study room, the library, and classrooms; on the second floor are the girls' dorms.

Our huge gymnasium.

A tour of the Groove High Campus

Our Dorm Room

Fashionably designed, well-lit, and well thought-out! Here's a small tour of the room . . .

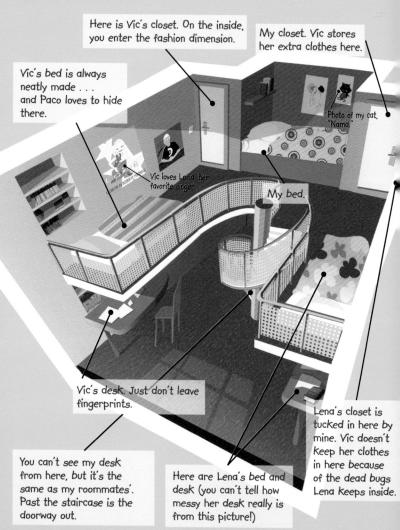

Here is Vic's closet. On the inside, you enter the fashion dimension.

My closet. Vic stores her extra clothes here.

Vic's bed is always neatly made . . . and Paco loves to hide there.

Photo of my cat, "Nama."

Vic loves Loria, her favorite singer.

My bed.

Vic's desk. Just don't leave fingerprints.

Lena's closet is tucked in here by mine. Vic doesn't keep her clothes in here because of the dead bugs Lena keeps inside.

You can't see my desk from here, but it's the same as my roommates'. Past the staircase is the doorway out.

Here are Lena's bed and desk (you can't tell how messy her desk really is from this picture!)

About the Author and Illustrator

Amélie Sarn: Amélie has two major flaws: excessive curiosity and a tendency to gorge herself. Not just on food, but on reading, travel, games, children, friends, and anything that makes her laugh. This gives her lots of material for stories! When her publisher asked her to write the stories of Zoe and the Groove Team, she revealed her dark side. Of all the characters in *Groove High*, she admits that her favorite is Kim!

Virgile Trouillot: With his feet on the ground, but his head forever in the clouds, Virgile spent his youth under the constant influence of cartoons, manga, and other comics. When he's not illustrating *Groove High* Books, Virgile develops animated series for *Planet Nemo*. Virgile spends time in his own version of a city zoo that's right in his apartment. His non-human companions include an army of ninja chinchillas that he has raised himself and many insects that science has not yet identified.

Web Sites

In order to ensure the safety and currency of recommended Internet links, Windmill maintains and updates an online list of sites. To access links to learn more about the *Groove High* characters and their adventures, please go to www.windmillbooks.com/weblinks and select this book's title.

For more great fiction and nonfiction, go to www.windmillbooks.com.